CECIL COUNTY
P9-CUK-181

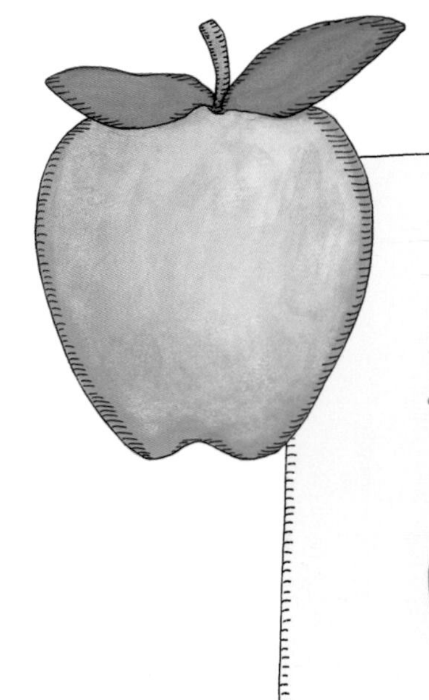

APPLES & ORANGES

going bananas with pairs

Sara Pinto

Typeset in Adobe Garamond, Lo-Type, and Pan Am
Art created with gouache, watercolor, and ink
Book design by Sue Schlabach

Published by Bloomsbury U.S.A. Children's Books
175 Fifth Avenue, New York, NY 10010
Distributed to the trade by Holtzbrinck Publishers

Library of Congress Cataloging-in-Publication Data
Pinto, Sara.
Apples and oranges : going bananas with pairs / by Sara Pinto. — 1st U.S. ed.
p. cm.
Summary: Presents pairs of related items, such as an apple and an orange or a bicycle
and a motorcycle, and asks why they are similar, while offering unexpected answers.
ISBN-13: 978-1-59990-103-9 • ISBN-10: 1-59990-103-X (hardcover)
ISBN-13: 978-1-59990-235-7 • ISBN-10: 1-59990-235-4 (reinforced)
[1. English language—Comparison—Fiction. 2. Questions and answers—Fiction.] I. Title.
PZ7.P6349Ap 2008 [E]—dc22 2007023548

First U.S. Edition 2008
Printed in China
1 3 5 7 9 10 8 6 4 2 (hardcover)
1 3 5 7 9 10 8 6 4 2 (reinforced)

To my kindergarten teacher, Mrs. Arlington,
wherever she may be

How are an apple and an orange alike?

They both don't wear glasses.

How are a bicycle and a motorcycle alike?

They both don’t work in a bank.

How are a cupcake and an ice-cream cone alike?

They both don't scuba dive.

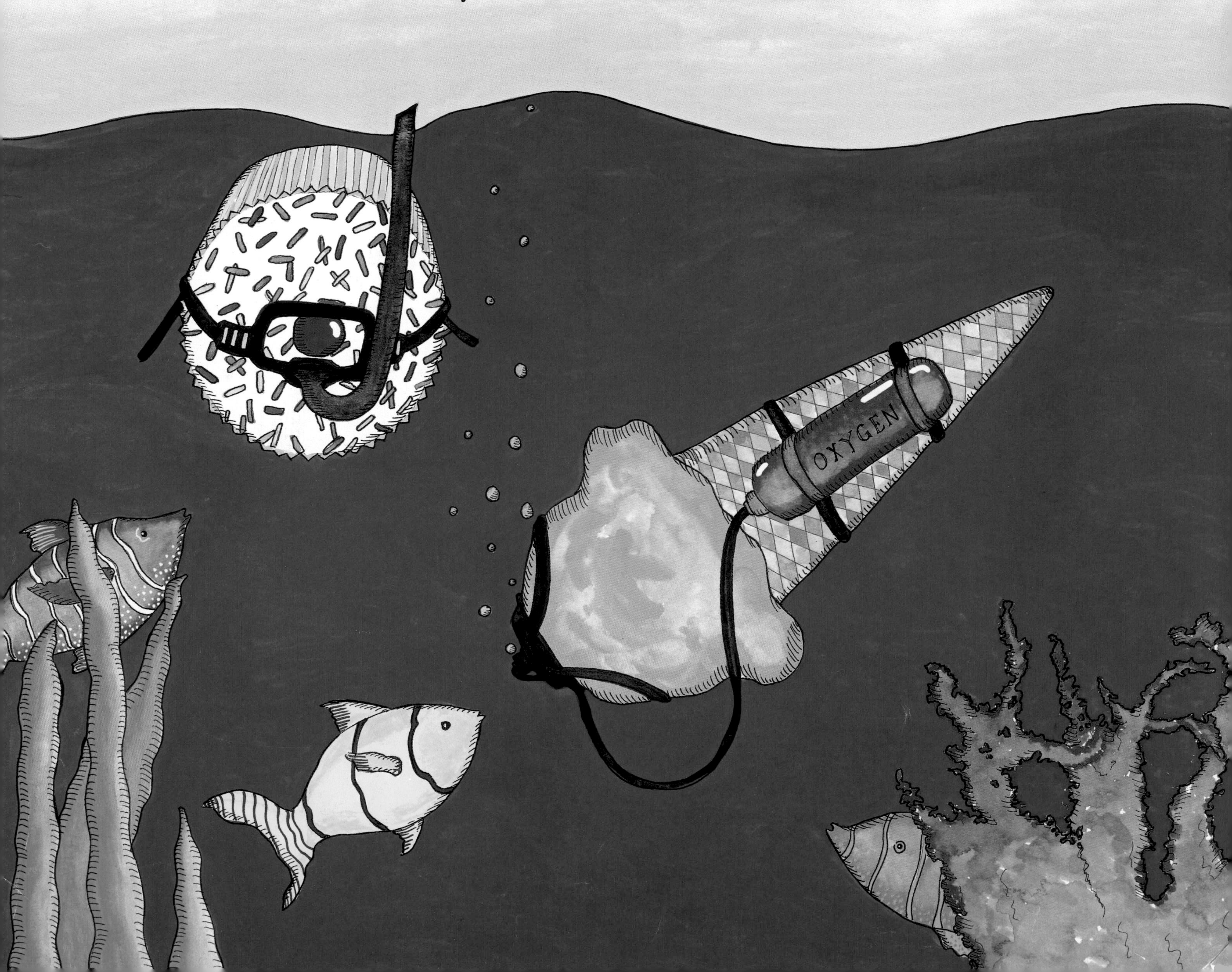

How are a bird and a kite alike?

They both don't talk on the phone.
Frank's Fruit & Flowers

How are a mug and a teacup alike?

They both don't ride in the rodeo.

How are a starfish and an octopus alike?

They both don't knit.

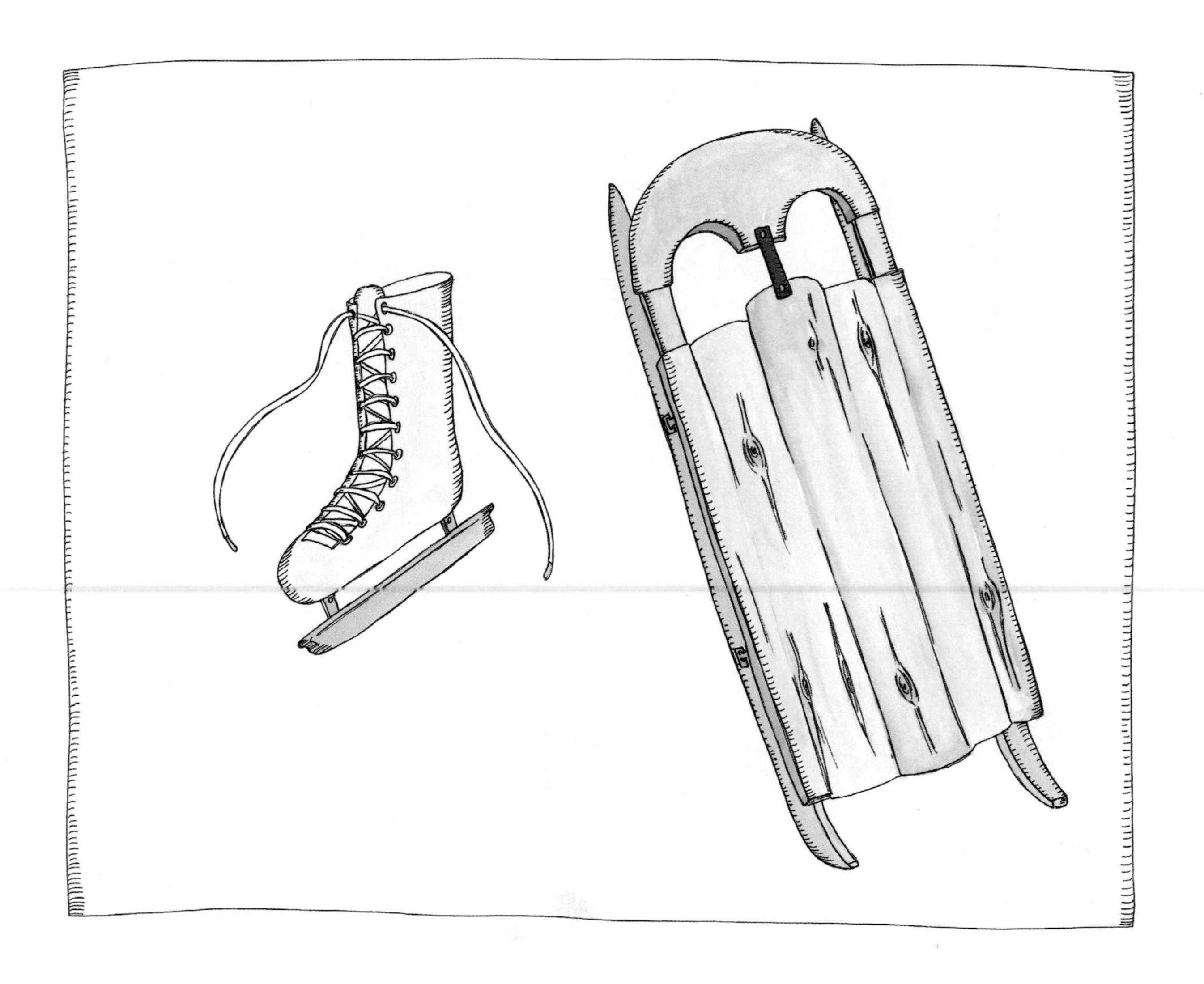

How are an ice skate and a sled alike?

They both don’t play jazz.

How are a rabbit and an armadillo alike?

They both don't work in a dentist's office.

How are a spoon and a fork alike?

They both don’t
dance in the ballet.

How are an accordion and a drum alike?

They both don't babysit.

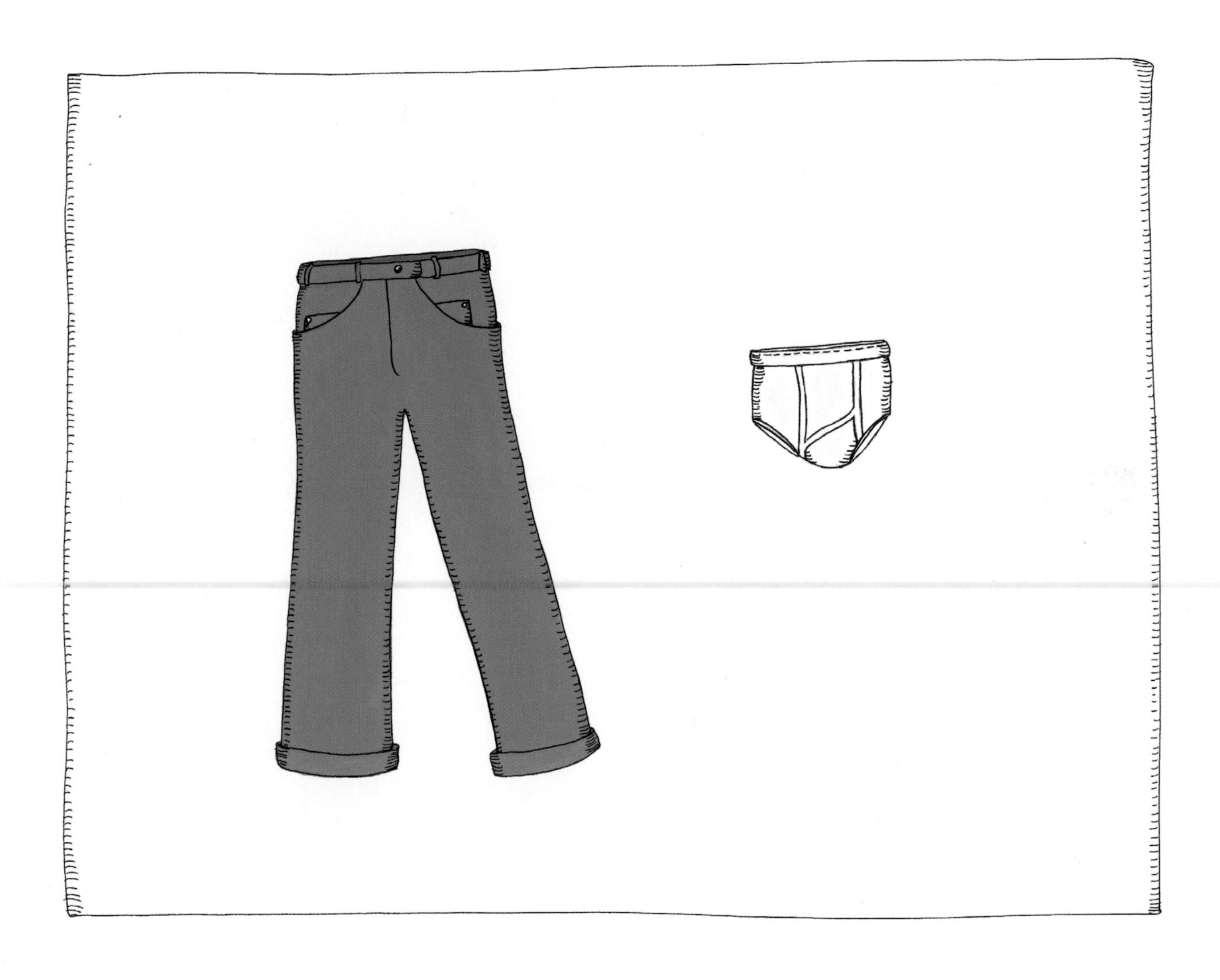

How are trousers and underpants alike?

They both don't make good hats.

How are a book and a letter alike?

They both don't go out for sushi.

How are an eggplant and an artichoke alike?

They both don't go to the carnival.

How are you and I alike?

We both don't . . .